our
generati♥n®

This is Tamera & Rashida's story.

# TAMERA & RASHIDA™

# A SUMMER OF RIDING

BY

SUSAN HUGHES

ILLUSTRATED BY GÉRALDINE CHARETTE

*An* Our Generation® *book*

MAISON BATTAT INC. *Publisher*

Our Generation® Books is a registered trademark of Maison Battat Inc.
Text copyright © 2018 by Susan Hughes
ISBN: 978-0-6929887-2-5
Printed in China

*Thank you to the Battat editorial team
for their help in creating this book,
especially editor Joanne Burke Casey
and designer Sandy Jacinto.*

Read all the adventures in the
**Our Generation®** Book Series

Read more about **Our Generation®** books and dolls online:
www.ogdolls.com

# CONTENTS

**EXTRA! EXTRA! READ ALL ABOUT IT!**
*Big words, wacky words, powerful words, funny words...*
*what do they all mean? They are marked with this symbol \*.*
*Look them up in the Glossary at the end of this book.*

## *Chapter One*

## ON THE ROAD TO HOME

I stroked my horse's nose, reassuring her.

"Don't worry, Corabelle," I said, "we'll soon be at our new home. Then we can get back to practicing for the end-of-summer show." I reached into the bag hanging in the trailer. "Here, have another carrot for lunch before we get back on the road," I told her.

It was our second stop today. My family had been traveling for more than a week. Each day we stopped once for lunch and several more times to check on Corabelle.

Our nights were spent in motels that also had stables attached. That way, Corabelle could stretch her legs a bit and sleep comfortably, too.

We'd left our home—well, our *old* home— in northern California on the first day after school ended. Since then, we'd driven every day in our pickup truck, pulling along our horse trailer.

Tomorrow we'll be in Connecticut. We're moving there because of my mom's work. She was offered a promotion* that meant transferring to New York City. She and my dad decided it would be a good move. They found the perfect home for us and Corabelle outside of the city, in Connecticut.

My sixteen-year-old sister, Lucy, was excited, of course. She saw this as a big adventure. But I wasn't sure about moving all the way across the country, leaving our old house and my neighborhood friends behind, *and* starting a new school.

"Rashida, you'll be fine," Lucy kept telling me. "Just wait until we get there."

Now we were only a day away from arriving, and I still felt nervous.

What about Corabelle and my dressage lessons? What about a riding instructor? I started riding four years ago, when I was five years old. I

10

loved it so much that, after some major pleading on my part, my parents agreed to buy me a horse.

That's my fabulous Corabelle, of course. She's a beautiful gray mare with a black mane and tail and black socks on all four of her legs. She is so gentle and smart!

I took lessons at the stable where I rode and improved a lot. I really loved it! After a while, Petra, my riding instructor, talked me into competing in a few shows, in the beginner dressage class. And I did OK.

Of course, that was mostly because of Corabelle. She had already been well-trained as a dressage horse before we got her. Basically, dressage is a type of riding where you ask your horse to do very precise* movements. At my level, that just means walking, trotting*, and halting* at specific spots in a ring. But it's important to do them as perfectly as possible.

In a competition*, the judges give each movement a score from zero to ten. Corabelle's an expert, but it was a matter of me learning the skills and learning how to communicate with her so we could work together.

As I started getting even more excited about dressage, Petra did some extra training with me. She worked with Corabelle and me on a lunge line*. That meant I didn't use reins* or have to worry about steering Corabelle. Petra did that. I could concentrate on how I was sitting on my horse. I became more balanced and relaxed. I could practice signaling* her using my legs.

But now, with the move…well, my horse would take some time to adjust to her new home, and so would my family and I.

I looked over at Lucy, who was digging into her chicken salad.

My sister and I would each be going to a new school in the fall. Lucy wasn't at all worried about it. She made new friends so easily. Not like me. She just did her own thing without caring what anyone thought, and everyone always seemed to think she was so cool.

For example, she's going to do a summer

12

internship* at a dress shop in our new town. She's passionate about fashion and wants to be a professional designer someday.

Lucy sews and sketches clothes all the time. After it was decided that we'd be moving to Pineridge, Connecticut, she and Mom searched online and found a little clothing boutique*. They got in touch with the owner and Lucy did an online interview. She was hired to work for them part-time this summer. She's amazing!

Me, on the other hand, I seem to have a bit of trouble making friends. I'm not sure why. I want to have friends—I want people to like me—but I'm not really outgoing, like Lucy.

I like to get to know people slowly. I don't know. Maybe other kids think I'm unfriendly.

"Don't worry about it, Rashida," Lucy told me one day. "Just be yourself."

"Yeah, well, maybe myself isn't the kind of girl other kids want to get to know," I said at the time.

Now I looked into Corabelle's beautiful brown eyes. "What do you think, Corabelle?" She snuffled*

at me with her velvety nose and I giggled.

My sister and I would miss our old friends, but I'd never had a special *best* friend because I spent so much time at the stable.

*Maybe I'll finally make a good friend once school begins,* I thought.

"But until then, I won't really have much time for anything other than preparing us for the show, will I, Corabelle?" I said to my horse.

After I found out exactly where we were moving, Dad had helped me research dressage shows online and we found one that would be held just one town over—right at the end of the summer.

It would take me all summer, riding and working with Corabelle, to make sure we did well in the show. Even so, I was actually looking forward to it. It was important for me to show everyone in my family how well I could ride.

"Come and eat, Rashida," Mom called.

"OK," I called back. I gave Corabelle a final pat on the nose, closed the trailer door, and headed to the picnic table.

# Chapter Two

## SECRET WISH

"Hey, Hugh!" I called, as I bounced into the kitchen for breakfast.

"Hey, Tamera," my brother answered.

"I'm just going to have some toast before I head out to the stable," I told him. "Want some?"

He nodded.

Our mom and dad own a riding stable here in Pineridge, Connecticut, and they have a few people on staff. But I help them out, too, especially in the summer—and school just ended this week!

I used to ride a lot and even competed a bit, mainly in jumping events. We have lots of jumps here and, because we have an indoor arena* and outdoor riding rings, I can practice all year-round. But recently, I'd stopped competing.

One reason is that Dad is a contractor*

who specializes in building stables and fencing, so he sometimes travels to oversee* his projects. For example, he's going to be gone a lot on weekdays *all* this summer. And Mom, who actually runs the farm day-to-day, has become too busy to be able to take me to shows anymore.

Not only do we rent out our own horses, we also rent out stalls to people who need to board* their horses and we offer the arena for practicing. We have a riding school and give lessons. Plus, every summer we run riding camps for kids.

I have to spend quite a bit of time helping out, which I don't mind, except it means that I can't meet up with friends from school very often. I used to have a really good friend who lived nearby, but she moved away in the spring.

Now that summer's here, I don't really have much time to spend with other people anyway, except the people who ride here. They're all nice, but most of them are either lots older than me or way too young.

"Hugh, I'm kind of excited!" I said. I poured

some orange juice for us both. "The family from California that's driving across the whole country to move here—the one with the horse that's going to board here…?"

I waited to see if he was listening. He didn't look up at me, but he turned his head a bit. I knew that meant he was following.

"Well, there are two girls. Mom says one is older, 16 or so, but the best part is that the younger girl, whose name is Rashida, is the same age as me and loves horses, too," I told him.

I put two pieces of whole wheat bread in the toaster and got the raspberry jam out of the refrigerator.

"I like horses, too," said Hugh with a nod.

"That's for sure," I agreed, with a grin. "So Rashida will be spending lots of time here at the stable because she wants to ride every day. Maybe…"

The toast popped up. I put two more pieces of bread in and brought the toast to the table. I tossed one onto Hugh's plate and we began spreading jam.

"Maybe…?" he prompted*. "Maybe what?"

Hugh is a year younger than me. He's really smart. He only wears blue clothes, he loves his teddy bear, and he has autism. That means his brain works a bit differently so he doesn't learn in quite the same way that I do, for example. He has trouble figuring out people just by watching them or listening to them.

Until last year, he never talked to me much about anything except his two favorite things: dinosaurs and rocks. And he hardly ever asked me any questions about myself. Mom and Dad said he had extra trouble communicating, but I sort of thought that might be usual for an eight-year-old kid.

For a while, I didn't feel like Hugh and I got along very well. I wasn't sure we had much in common. But ever since he started riding a few months ago, things between us changed. Now we have something we both love: horses.

Hugh is crazy about them. He reads all about

them. He knows way more than I do about them! So we talk to each other quite a bit more—about horses, but sometimes about other things, too.

"Tamera?" Hugh spoke up.

I was about to tell him that I hoped Rashida would become my new friend.

I knew I shouldn't get my hopes up. After all, we could be totally different or have completely opposite personalities*. Or each of us might be too busy to hang out much. But it would be great if we really hit it off and became best buddies!

"Tamera?" Hugh repeated. "Toast's up." He pointed at the toaster. "Can you get it for me, please?"

"Sure," I said, and laughed. The moment for confiding* was gone, and I was a bit relieved. Hoping Rashida might become my best buddy could just be my secret wish.

## Chapter Three

## WELCOME TO ROUND-THE-RING STABLES

"We're almost there," said Lucy, peering at the GPS screen on the dashboard.

We'd gotten off the highway and had been driving down country roads for about 20 minutes.

All our furniture and Mom's car had been sent ahead of us to our new house, and we knew it would be there, waiting for us. But first we had to make sure we got Corabelle settled in *her* new home.

We'll be boarding her at a stable that's also in Pineridge. We'd heard good things about it, and Mom had said it was close enough to our new house for me to ride my bike there.

That's good, because I want to spend every day there this summer, getting ready for competing.

"It should be coming up on the left," said

Lucy, pointing.

Sure enough, I could see a farmhouse, a long stable, a couple of outdoor riding rings, and what looked like an indoor arena. Farther off I saw some fenced fields and a hill with one single tree up on top.

We turned into the driveway and pulled up to the unloading area. As I jumped out, my heart was pounding.

Right away, a girl who looked about my age came up to greet us. "Welcome to Round-the-Ring Stables. I'm Tamera," she said, and she even put her hand out. Mom and Dad grinned and shook her hand—they like kids with good manners.

Mom introduced Lucy and me.

"We've been expecting Corabelle," said Tamera. "I just finished getting her stall ready. I can't wait to meet her!"

*I guess Tamera helps out here maybe,* I thought. She seemed really calm and cool.

A cheerful woman hurried out of the stable. "I see you've met Tamera," she said. "I'm her mother, and our family are the proud owners of Round-the Ring Stables!"

We all said hello and introduced ourselves.

"Now let's see how that horse of yours is, Rashida," she said, "and introduce her to her new 'home sweet home.'"

"OK," I said, feeling a bit tongue-tied*.

We headed to the back of the trailer. Corabelle is pretty good about being in the trailer and getting in and out. We'd had to load and unload her quite a few times since we left home. But I always worry about unloading her. She has to back down the ramp.

We've practiced lots with her, especially when we weren't in a rush to go somewhere, and we've taught her to move slowly and steadily. But still, it always seems to me like it's scary, backing down without being able to see where you're going. Corabelle has to really trust us to do that.

It was obvious that Corabelle was a bit nervous. She tossed her head around inside the trailer once, twice.

"Would you like me to go and untie her?" Tamera asked Dad.

"Thank you, young lady," Dad replied.

"My mom taught me about trailering horses," Tamera said, with a smile. "I'm young, but I have quite a bit of experience—probably like your daughter, Rashida."

Tamera went in the side door of the trailer. She untied Corabelle from the trailer, attached the lead rope that Dad had handed her to Corabelle's halter*, and then Dad swung open the back doors.

I went inside the trailer and took the lead rope from Tamera while Dad lowered the ramp. Slowly, I backed Corabelle down the ramp, and— ta-da! She was officially in her new home, safe and sound.

"Oh, she's a beauty!" Tamera's mom said.

"She is!" agreed Tamera. "We're happy to have you here, Corabelle!"

Then Tamera offered to show Lucy and Mom around while Dad and I went along with Tamera's mother and Corabelle to make sure

Corabelle was OK in her new stall.

As we walked her over, I glanced back. Lucy wasn't using her wheelchair. She didn't use it all the time. Sometimes she used her forearm crutches instead. Tamera was chatting happily with Lucy.

*What are they talking about?* I wondered. Lucy is very friendly and she makes everyone feel comfortable somehow. Whenever she meets people, everyone wants to talk with her and get to know her, like Tamera was doing.

Lucy never needs to think about what she wants to say before saying it, the way I do. I'm worried about saying the wrong thing; she doesn't worry at all.

For a moment I wondered if maybe *I* could become friends with Tamera, but no, I reminded myself—it was more important for me to focus on Corabelle.

Tamera's mom led us into the stable and put Corabelle in her stall. We took off her travel bandages*, gave her some fresh water, and soon she was settled in. Then Dad headed back to the

26

pickup truck.

"Bye, Corabelle," I whispered. "I'll come back and see you tomorrow, don't you worry!"

When I returned to the unloading area, Dad had driven the truck to a parking area near the barn. He had unhitched* the trailer from the truck and parked it so we could use the truck without needing to pull the trailer around.

I hoped that the next time we would need it again would be when we were heading to the big show, Corabelle and me!

"OK, gang, now let's head out to settle into *our* new home!" said Mom.

We all said goodbye to Tamera and her mom. Tamera reassured us that she'd check in on Corabelle in a little while, just to make sure she was settled down.

"Tamera is so nice," said Lucy, as we drove away. "And all the horses here at Round-the-Ring are beautiful!"

I looked back at the stable through the truck window. Tamera was there, waving goodbye.

## Chapter Four

## JUST TRYING TO HELP

It had been about a week and a half since Rashida arrived here with her horse, Corabelle. I'd been doing my regular routine around the stable: grooming the riding school horses, helping to feed and water them, mucking out* the stalls, and helping with the riding camp.

But I was a bit disappointed. Rashida's sister is friendly, but Rashida didn't seem very interested in making friends with me.

For example, the day after Corabelle got here, Mom and I went out to greet Rashida after her dad dropped her off. We wanted her to feel comfortable.

"We've got an indoor arena, but we mostly only use that in the winter or when the weather is extremely bad in other seasons," Mom told

Rashida. "We're beginning our summer riding camps, but the riding camp only uses ring A. It's also used for jumping."

"You can use ring B," I explained. "It's mainly for dressage and usually only boarders, like you, use it. Sometimes you'll find you have the whole ring to yourself."

I added, "And Ring C is for therapeutic riding* lessons."

Rashida just nodded and said OK. She seemed in a hurry to get to Corabelle.

Off and on over the next few days, while I was working around the farm, I saw Rashida with her horse. She really was good with her. She took her time with Corabelle, making sure she got settled in alright.

The first day, she talked to her horse and groomed* her, mainly just spending time with her. She put her on a lead and walked her down the driveway and back, letting her see and get used to the place. Rashida's dad rode his bike over and brought her lunch that day, and the two of them

30

ate together.

The next day, Rashida tacked up* and took Corabelle out on the lead again for a while. She walked her down to the road and back again. The next two or three days, she took her into Ring B, which was empty each time, and walked her around the ring for a bit.

On Monday this week, I noticed her mount up* and do some easy riding. She walked and did some trotting. She switched directions a few times, and she rode in circles—first big ones and then small ones.

While Rashida was training with Corabelle, I'd been doing my stable chores and also helping with the therapeutic riding, which I do a few times a week. I really like being in the ring with the kids and the horses, especially when my brother is riding.

When I'm 13, I'll be able to actually assist with the horses and riders. For now I can be useful by giving a hand with the equipment in the ring and going on errands for the instructors and other volunteers when they're busy. Like I was doing today.

When the afternoon's therapeutic riding lessons were done, I glanced over at Ring B. Rashida hadn't looked my way even once. She didn't seem at all interested. She seemed so focused on her own horse.

Anyway, it looked like she was done with her training session, too. She was walking Corabelle on a loose rein again.

So I put the equipment away and went over to the fence.

As Rashida was leaving the ring, I called to her.

"Do you need some help grooming and watering Corabelle, Rashida?" I offered. I hoped that if we spent some time together, maybe, just maybe, we might find out we like each other.

She seemed to be thinking it over. Then she said, "No, thanks." She didn't really look me in the eye when she spoke.

I felt kind of hurt. Maybe she thought I was

being pushy? I wasn't sure.

Anyway, I just smiled and said, "OK, maybe some other time!"

But hmmm…maybe I won't actually ask again.

## Chapter Five

## AN IDEA FOR LUCY

We'd been in our new home about ten days or so. A few days ago, my family and I checked out the town and went for some drives through the countryside, just to get the lay of the land*, as my Dad liked to say.

I still feel sad about leaving my old friends. When Mom gave me some computer time, I'd emailed back and forth with some of them. I'd also sent Petra an email to let her know I was starting to work on our new training schedule.

Both Lucy and I had been really busy. My sister started working every morning at the dress shop, and I'd been spending most of my time with Corabelle.

Except for the first morning when Dad dropped me off, I'd been riding my bike over to the stables.

Mom and Dad aren't able to drive me very often. Mom has to leave early each morning to drive or take the train to work in New York City. Dad works from home but brings Lucy back and forth to her job in town.

It's great to be able to be at the stables every day so I can focus on getting Corabelle—and myself—ready for the competition.

I'd been thinking about this for months, ever since my parents first got in touch with Tamera's mom and we chose to bring Corabelle to Round-the-Ring Stables. We'd reviewed their safety rules and agreed to them all.

Tamera's mom explained that I am old enough to ride on my own with a little supervision. I promised to always let an instructor know when Corabelle and I would be in the ring so someone could keep an eye on us.

Last week, the day after I arrived, the head instructor, Nora, met with me and went over all the safety rules again. She invited me to join any of

36

the group lessons, and I explained that I might, but that Petra and I had also set up a simple training program that Corabelle and I could do on our own.

So I spent that first week settling Corabelle in. This week, I began to practice with her in Ring B, preparing for the show.

I remember Petra first explaining dressage to me as sort of like a dance routine. A rider and her horse do a set pattern of movements. For example, we walk, trot, canter*, and halt, in circles, straight lines, or even on diagonals*. Letters and numbers placed along the sides and ends of the ring help the rider keep track of where and when to do the movements.

That's what Corabelle and I are beginning to work hard at now: learning the patterns in our competition test and doing them as perfectly as we can. We end up by walking down the centerline toward the judges. Then we halt, and I salute.

I keep a copy of the exact movements in my pocket so if I need a reminder, I can peek at them as I ride. But I'll have to memorize them in time for the show!

I work on the memorizing in between riding Corabelle. During this time I also groom her, clean her saddle*, and muck out her stall.

Sometimes I sit and read in the stable while she's resting. I always have a book with me, often a story about a horse or a dog, or one of my dressage books.

Several times a day, I check in with the instructors, and they're really encouraging. They watch me when I ride, and comment on my riding style or try to give me tips.

Also, the owners' daughter, Tamera, has asked me a few times if I need help with anything, which was really nice of her.

But I wasn't sure, so I said no. Corabelle is so calm and experienced. She and I learned the basics of our dressage test with Petra, and we're doing OK practicing on our own.

I'm a bit anxious about remembering the dressage "dance" from beginning to end without forgetting any of it *and* doing the movements just right. But I shouldn't really need anyone to help me with that.

Tamera seems so calm and so confident that I kind of don't want her to know I feel uncertain about the test. Silly of me...but that's just me.

A few days ago, I was surprised to see Lucy arrive at the stable with Mom. Lucy told me she wanted to watch me train for a bit, and she did watch. But then she headed over to ring C to watch the therapeutic riding class. I was surprised to see Tamera there, too, helping out.

Today, Dad brought Lucy by the stables again. I'd just finished my ride, so I put Corabelle in her stall, put away her tack, and went to say hi to my sister. She was leaning on the rail at ring C, watching the therapeutic riding again.

There were horses with riders of all different ages. Three people walked with each horse, one leading the horse and two others walking on either side of the rider. One person seemed to be the instructor. She talked a lot and demonstrated the activities.

Two of the riders began following their instructor's actions, holding their hands out wide to the side. The other riders were holding hoops. They held them out to the side with one hand, and then above their heads with two hands.

Tamera was in the ring, holding the extra hoops. When one of the riders dropped a hoop, Tamera hurried over, picked it up, and handed it to the rider's instructor.

Just then, the lesson finished up. Tamera saw us, waved, and came over.

"All these kids have some kind of cognitive*, physical*, or emotional* special needs*. That's my brother, Hugh, riding Adobe," she said proudly. "The movement of the horse helps him in lots of ways, like with balance and coordination. And he's learning to communicate with the horse."

Lucy sighed. "I wish I could ride," she said, which surprised me. Totally.

"Well, why don't you give it a try?" asked Tamera.

Lucy looked at her and then at me.

"Come on, Lucy!" Tamera encouraged her. "Why not?"

Lucy thought for a moment. I did, too. Something bothered me about this idea.

"Lucy's sort of busy with other things," I explained to Tamera. "She wants to be a fashion designer. She's helping out at a dress shop, and she likes to spend lots of time sketching designs and…"

Lucy and Tamera looked at me a little funny.

"It's good exercise," Lucy said, slowly. "You know Dad's always reminding me to exercise more. And…I think it looks fun."

"OK," I said, frowning. "It is fun. Lots of fun. I was only trying to help."

Dad came over, and right away, Lucy asked him if she could try the therapeutic riding. Dad looked surprised, too, but really pleased.

"Great idea!" he said. "Let's discuss it with

Mom. I'm sure she'll agree."

Tamera grinned. She said she'd get them all the forms they needed to fill out and she hurried away. I headed to the stable to groom Corabelle.

*Why do I feel weird about this?* I wondered. *What does it matter if Lucy wants to learn to ride?*

And why did it matter to me if Tamera was interested in helping Lucy learn to ride? I didn't really have time to make a new friend anyway.

## *Chapter Six*

### TIME TO TALK

It was exciting to think that Rashida's sister would go riding for the first time next week. I remembered the first time Hugh sat on a horse. I didn't think we'd ever get him to dismount*!

I thought Rashida would also be happy about the idea when I suggested it, but she hadn't seemed to be. She couldn't be angry with me for suggesting that her sister try riding, could she? That wouldn't make any sense.

Something about me seemed to be bothering her, though. All this week, anytime I'd gone over to Rashida to talk to her, she'd found a reason to walk away. I was pretty sure she was avoiding me. Maybe she'd simply decided she didn't like me.

*Sigh!* I'm trying so hard to help Mom out around the stable and to seem confident with all the clients, when deep down I feel uncertain a lot of the time. Mom works lots of hours, day and night, to keep the business going. It's actually going along really well, so I'm not too worried about that.

What I *am* uncertain about is whether I'll ever have a friend of my own, someone to share my love of horses with, someone I can confide in. I'd love a friend who I could let down my guard* with, someone who I didn't mind knowing that I'm not really as confident as I might seem.

I had hoped Rashida might be that friend. *Should I try talking to her again?* Then, no, I decided. I wouldn't worry about it for now. I had lots of things to do to take my mind off that.

So I carried on as usual helping out around the stable—and twice this week I was able to ride! Marjorie, the jumping instructor, had extra room in her class. Mom wanted me to exercise Amiga, our eight-year-old chestnut mare, so I got to join in on the jumping class one day.

Another day, I got to ride Domino, one of the boarder ponies, because his owner couldn't come and wanted to make sure the pony was ridden.

And now today, everything was sorted out so that Lucy could have her first riding lesson.

Rashida's mom and dad arrived with Rashida and Lucy. Instead of heading straight for Corabelle as usual, Rashida hung around. She had to be excited to see her sister ride for the first time!

Nora led Adobe over to Lucy. Adobe is the bay* pony that Hugh had been riding. Two of our volunteer sidewalkers* went with her.

Soon Lucy had on a riding helmet. Next she went up the ramp in her wheelchair and after some instruction from Nora, and some help from the volunteers, she was able to mount the pony.

I went to stand with Rashida and her mother to watch Lucy's first lesson.

Nora showed Lucy how to hold the reins and how to position her legs. There was a helper on each side of Lucy to make sure she was steady and balanced. And then, Adobe walked on and— Lucy was riding! Lucy had a huge grin on her face.

"I never thought I'd see this day," said

Rashida's dad, reaching for Rashida's hand.

"Me either," said Rashida. She looked really happy for her sister.

"Amazing!" I said. Rashida smiled at me, and I smiled back.

Since Lucy's first lesson, I'd helped out with three more therapeutic riding classes. Hugh was in one of them, and Lucy was in the other two. She kept saying that Rashida was the real rider in the family and that she was just doing it for fun. Isn't that the best reason of all? She seemed to really love it!

This morning, Mom had gone down to her office in the stable early, but Hugh and I had breakfast with Dad. He didn't have to leave early today, so he made us blueberry pancakes.

After we ate, Dad asked Hugh if he wanted to go with him to his new worksite, and Hugh said sure. So Hugh grabbed his dinosaurs and the two of them jumped in the truck and headed out.

I went out to the barns to clean out the stalls, which took up most of the morning.

In the afternoon, I got to exercise one of the boarder's ponies, and I even managed to spend an hour at my favorite place in the world—the top of Maple Hill!

It's so peaceful up there. And today the summer sun was really beating down. So after I sat in the shade of the maple tree, I soared back and forth for a while in the wooden tree swing, enjoying the breeze I made.

I was heading back to the stable to water the horses when I stopped by the ring to watch Rashida. She was mainly walking and trotting. As usual, she was concentrating really hard, turning at particular letters, frowning a bit. And as usual I don't think she even noticed I was there.

That was OK, I guess. She *was* here to ride, after all. Still, I decided I'd give it another shot, even if she turned me down again. I really wanted to keep trying to be her friend. So when she took a break, I went to talk with her.

"You look so good at dressage," I said. "I only know a little about it. I took lessons last year and we did some very basic exercises. We did a little jumping, too, and some barrel racing*. I liked them all, but I wasn't really good at any one of them."

Rashida didn't say anything for a moment or two. She didn't seem to want to talk to me. Oh well. Maybe making friends just isn't important to her right now. *Maybe we're just too different to be friends.*

Then she said, "Thanks," and added, "You know, I'm preparing for this show. I'm trying hard to improve."

I nodded. "OK, well, I know Nora and the other riding instructors are helping you out a bit. And I'm not an expert on dressage. But please let me know if I can give you a hand at all."

She smiled. Again, she thought for a moment before she said, "I can't think of any way that you could help."

Now, sometimes Hugh says things like that, and his words sound harsh, but I know Hugh doesn't mean them that way. And it's helped me to see that other people also sometimes say things that sound harsh without meaning to. So I decided to give Rashida the benefit of the doubt* and not take her words in the way they sounded.

"Thank you, though," Rashida added.

I said, "That's OK," and turned to go.

Then Rashida said, "Hang on, Tamera." To my surprise, she dismounted from Corabelle. She sort of took a deep breath.

I reached out and stroked Corabelle's nose, just to give her some time.

"Tamera, can *you* think of any way you could help me? At all?" Rashida asked. "Because I really, really want to improve, but I'm not sure if I am."

"Oh!" I said. "That's great. Sure, just give me some time to think of something. I'm sure I'll find a way to help."

She relaxed a little. "Thanks," she said, with a tiny smile. "See you tomorrow?"

"See you tomorrow," I agreed.

## Chapter Seven

## CORABELLE SAYS THANK YOU

"Corabelle, can you believe it?" I asked. "You know I've been kind of grumpy with Tamera, and yesterday, she asked me if she could help us prepare for the dressage competition! It was nice of her, right?"

Corabelle blinked her long eyelashes. She gazed at me with her beautiful brown eyes.

Nothing I told her ever seemed to surprise Corabelle. I always felt better after talking to her.

I thought about Hugh and Lucy, and then I thought about *all* the riders I know. *Maybe riding horses is therapeutic for everyone, including me. There's just something magical about it.*

I finished grooming Corabelle in her stall and headed for my bike. I was almost hoping Tamera would forget about our conversation. I was a bit embarrassed about it.

But she came running up to me as I wheeled my bike to the gate.

"I've got it!" Tamera said. "I think I know how I can help you! What if I use my Mom's video camera to shoot a video of you riding Corabelle? Mom says it's alright with her and she even lent me a flash memory card*.

"I'll film you and Corabelle from each end of the ring. Then you can take the memory card home, watch the video and see how your posture* looks, how well you're keeping in rhythm, how straight Corabelle is traveling—everything!"

I thought about her idea closely. *Would this be the best way to improve our dressage performance?* Tamera waited patiently.

"That sounds like a really good idea," I said, finally.

Tamera grinned.

When we met up later in the day, Tamera

filmed as I rode Corabelle through the whole competition test. Then she simply popped the memory card out of the video camera and handed it to me.

"Thank you," I told her. "I'll watch it tonight." With a smile, I added, "And Corabelle says thank you, too!"

I watched Tamera's video just before bedtime that night and again the next morning. It gave me lots of ideas about what I needed to concentrate on to improve. Tamera's idea had been really clever!

૮♃ ♃ა

A few days later, Tamera and I were watching a group of young riders from the summer camp learn barrel racing. Well, they were supposed to be practicing weaving* in and out of the barrels.

But one of the ponies just refused to obey her rider. She kept running out, instead of weaving through the barrels. The rider, a boy who looked about seven years old, complained. "Tiny doesn't know how to do it."

The instructor assured him that the pony knew how and that he needed to be a little more assertive*.

"Show me," the boy demanded.

"I'm too big and tall to ride Tiny," the instructor explained. She called Tamera over.

A few minutes later, Tamera put on her hard hat. Tiny's rider dismounted and Tamera climbed aboard the pony. Off she went, weaving through the barrels like the wind!

She did an amazing demonstration*. I couldn't believe how good she was at barrel racing. And she'd told me she wasn't really good at any one thing!

"You're great at barrel racing, Tamera!" I told her, enthusiastically. "There's going to be some barrel racing at the show I'm going to next month. If you practiced more you could be the best in your age category!"

But Tamera laughed. "Maybe," she said. "But I just don't want to."

"Why don't you try?" I asked. "Are you

afraid of losing?"

Then I thought, *Oh no. That wasn't a very nice thing to say. I was just starting to feel like we might be friends. Now I've gone and said something that might hurt Tamera's feelings.*

But Tamera just shrugged and smiled. "No, it isn't that. Really," she said. She paused. I thought she was about to go on and say more about it, but then her mother called to her.

So she just shrugged again, and said, "See you later, Rashida!"

## Chapter Eight

## ON TOP OF MAPLE HILL

I was enjoying spending time with Rashida and getting to know her. Sure, she was intense* about her riding, especially about competing in the dressage show. She talked a lot about it and worried about how she and Corabelle could improve. But she also started smiling more and asking me questions about Hugh and therapeutic riding.

This week, I had videoed Rashida two more times. Each time, she told me she was really grateful for my help. It's funny—she never just bursts out saying thank you.

I figured out that she just likes to choose her words carefully before she speaks. She seems to want to say things just right. And that's OK with me.

Today, when Rashida asked me to look at the videos with her and help her evaluate her progress, I made a suggestion. "Would you like to come up to the top of Maple Hill with me? Why don't we go at noon. We'll bring our lunches. We can sit under my favorite tree and look at the videos there."

After a moment, she gave a nod and smiled.

We had such a great time together. Rashida told me she sees why it's my favorite place because it's so beautiful up there! We sat on the swing for a bit first. Then we spread out a picnic blanket and ate and talked about all kinds of things, including our families, just like friends do.

I told Rashida a bit more about Hugh and Rashida told me how much she admires her sister. She said Lucy's so confident and doesn't worry about anything, not even starting a new school this fall. Rashida hinted that she was a bit worried about that herself.

"Don't worry," I told her. "It's a small school, and there's only one class for each grade. We'll be in the same class, and I'll introduce you to all the kids."

Right away, she looked relieved.

We began watching the videos together, and Rashida was quick to spot exactly what she needed help with.

Then she asked, "Tamera, can you help me in another way?" She hesitated and chose her words. "Can you watch me while I ride? Tell me if Corabelle's walk is straighter? Maybe you could even clap in time with Corabelle so we can check if her trot is balanced and even?"

"Sure!" I said, enthusiastically. I couldn't believe she'd actually asked me for more help.

So it gave me an idea. I'd noticed Rashida sneaking peeks at the therapeutic riding classes lately. Before she didn't seem aware of them at all. Since Lucy started classes she seemed more interested.

"Rashida, maybe I can ask you for some help, too," I said, cautiously.

"OK," she replied. "What is it?"

"Would you mind helping out with the therapeutic riding lessons this afternoon? We could really use a hand. Lots of our volunteers go on summer vacations and we end up being shorthanded*. Like today, for example," I explained. "I think Lucy is riding today, too."

Without thinking twice, Rashida nodded. "Sure, I will," she said.

So we headed back down to the stable for the afternoon, and at four o'clock, when it was time for the therapeutic riding lessons, Rashida's dad and Lucy showed up, along with the other riders, and so did Rashida.

I explained to her what she needed to do. She helped me tack up the horses and bring them out to the yard. We made sure to have plenty of water on hand during the lesson for the riders and instructors, because it was an especially hot day. And we did lots of running for equipment.

Rashida and Lucy grinned at each other a lot. At one point, Lucy called to Rashida, "It's so funny to see you on the ground while I'm the one up here on the horse!"

When the lesson was over, Rashida talked to her father for a bit and then she came over to me.

"Tamera, I'd love to help out with the therapeutic riding classes for the rest of the summer. Dad says it's OK," Rashida said. "That is, if it's OK with you and your mom."

"Thank you," I said. "That would be great."

I felt so good. I'd solved one of our work problems and I'd made a friend happy, too!

## Chapter Nine

## MEGA-INTENSE!

It turned out that I really enjoyed helping with the therapeutic riding, so I started doing it regularly. This week I helped out three times. I was a "gofer"—which meant if one of the riders or volunteers needed an extra piece of equipment or wanted to talk to one of the parents, I was the person to "go for" it!

I felt good about it. I knew I'd been thinking about myself a lot recently. I needed to think about doing things for other people, too.

I owed it to Tamera. She had asked me to help out with the therapeutic riding, and I knew she really *did* need help.

But I think that, somehow, she also knew it might be good for *me* to lend a hand, and that I might learn something from it. And she was right.

I'd just put Corabelle out in one of the fields to graze* and was headed back to the stable yard.

As I passed the therapeutic ring where Lucy was riding, I stopped and watched her for a moment. Suddenly, I remembered how I had responded when Tamera first suggested that Lucy try the therapeutic riding. I had been so selfish! I was ashamed of myself.

Then Lucy waved at me, and I waved back, grinning.

I decided I had to talk to Tamera, now. I had to explain why I'd been acting this way.

I'd seen her going into the stable, so I headed in, and there she was, in one of the stalls.

"Tamera, can I talk to you for a minute?" I asked.

"Sure," she answered. "I've just finished grooming Button."

She gave the white mare a pat on the shoulder and came out of her stall, closing the stall door behind her.

I began right away, not wanting to lose my

nerve. "Tamera, I've been so focused on Corabelle and my own riding…it's been the only thing I've cared about." I took a breath. "I guess I've been a bit jealous of all the attention my parents give to Lucy." I didn't dare to look Tamera in the eyes.

"Lucy is so smart, and she works so hard but she never complains. She deserves my parents' attention! And it's not that my parents ignore me. But I just feel like I need to prove to them that I can be really special, too," I explained.

"So, if I do well at the horse show, it will make me feel special, too, and everyone else in my family might think I'm special."

There. I was done.

Tamera thought quietly for a long time. Did she hate me? Maybe.

"You know, my parents always tell me that I'm special, like my brother but in a different way," Tamera said. "I bet your parents feel that way about you, too—you *and* your sister. I think they'll be happy for you if you win the competition, but I don't think their feelings for you will change.

"And you know what? If you don't win this summer, you can practice all winter and then try again next summer. You're only going to get better and better." Tamera grinned. "I have the videos to prove it!

"It's OK to want to win! It's OK to want to be really good at something," Tamera said. Then, in a quiet voice, she asked, "Can I tell you something?"

"Sure," I said.

"You're right that I'm not too crazy about competing," Tamera said. "I like doing all kinds of riding and I don't want to focus on just one kind. I like jumping, but I also like dressage, and barrel racing, and just going on relaxing trail rides*!

"Another reason is because my brother started riding last year. It's kind of amazing really. You know Hugh has autism."

I nodded.

"Well, my parents and I always knew he liked being with the horses, but he'd never really shown any interest in riding," Tamera explained.

"Then one day, Gordon, who boards his horse with us, asked Hugh if he'd like to sit on his horse—and Hugh said yes! We were surprised, because usually Hugh didn't even like to talk to people outside our family.

"Anyway, when Mom said it was OK, Gordon helped him up and led his horse around, with Hugh onboard. He had the biggest grin on his face!"

"I can just picture it!" I said.

"Mom and Dad saw how much Hugh loved it, and how it helped him to connect with other people. We began offering therapeutic riding lessons here at our stable," Tamera continued.

"It turned out there was a big need for it in our community, and the lessons filled up quickly. Mom and Dad needed me to help out more. So I gave up my regular riding lessons and training for competitions—and I totally didn't mind," Tamera added quickly. "I'm happy that I can ride and even join in on a lesson whenever I get a chance."

Finally I understood, and I believed her.

69

"There is something I do want to get good at though," Tamera said. "It just isn't to do with horses."

"What is it?" I asked, although I was pretty sure I already knew.

She looked at me cautiously, like she thought I might laugh, like she was trying to decide whether to trust me. "I want to work with kids who have autism," she said. "Kids like my brother."

I nodded.

"It makes me feel happy to see Hugh smile and enjoy himself, and to find something that he's good at," Tamera explained. "I think I want to help other people with special needs find ways to be confident, too. Whatever that way is."

I nodded again. "You'd be great at that," I said.

For a moment, Tamera and I both looked at each other. I think we were both surprised that we had so much to tell each other—and happy about it, too! We burst out laughing.

"How intense was that?" she said, giggling.

70

"Totally intense!" I replied, grinning like crazy.

"Super intense!"

"Mega-intense!"

We both giggled some more.

"Hey, want to go watch the last few minutes of my amazing sister's riding lesson?" I suggested.

"Good idea," Tamera agreed, and as we headed off together, I couldn't remember being happier.

## *Chapter Ten*

## A NIGHT FOR HAVING FUN

There was only a week left before Rashida's show. She'd been helping out with the therapeutic riding a few times a week, but was still practicing lots with Corabelle, too.

I'd been doing all my regular farm work, plus doing a little riding of my own—and helping Rashida with her dressage training.

Dad had taken a few afternoons off so he could do some fun summer things with Hugh and me. We went on a long bike ride, we hung out in the river nearby, splashing in its little waterfall, and we even went go-cart riding.

On Wednesday, Rashida and I were enjoying some cold water while she waited for her mom to pick her up.

"Hey, Tamera," she asked, suddenly, "do

you want to come for a sleepover at my house tonight? I'm sure it would be OK with my parents."

"Sure," I agreed. Then I paused. "I guess it would give us more time to talk about your riding and the show."

Rashida laughed. "No way," she said firmly. "We'd have to agree: neither of us is allowed to talk about the show. This will be a night off from all that for both of us. A night just for having fun! Deal?"

"Deal!" I agreed.

"Oh, and bring along a sleeping bag, if you have one," Rashida added.

Of course Mom agreed it was OK, and she and Hugh drove me over later. Hugh was also excited because Mom was taking him to a movie to make the night special for him, too.

After I had dinner with Rashida and her family, Rashida said, "Tamera, I set up our tent in the backyard the other day. Want to sleep outside in it tonight?"

"Oh, so that's why you asked me to bring

along my sleeping bag!" I said. "Sure! I've never slept in a tent before."

We hurried up to Rashida's room with my overnight bag, and we put our pajamas on and brushed our teeth.

Rashida threw several things into her bag: a pack of cards, flashlights, and some board games. Then we grabbed our bags, the sleeping bags, and a few pillows each, and we called goodnight to her family.

"Don't forget to bring the snacks!" Lucy reminded us.

A pretty green and purple tent was already set up in the backyard. It was plenty big enough for both of us. We settled in for a night of playing games, stargazing, and telling ghost stories.

Well, it turned out I was the only one who knew any ghost stories—and when I told them, Rashida actually got a bit nervous! So I changed the ending of the third one to make it funny, not scary. It was more fun making my friend laugh than making her scared!

Rashida and I were both sorry when we started yawning. Neither of us wanted to go to sleep. Finally, we just couldn't keep our eyes open any longer. We crawled into our sleeping bags and began to nod off.

"Tamera?" Rashida whispered in the dark. "I know we said we wouldn't talk about riding, but...can I ask you something?"

"Sure," I replied.

"Will you come to the show next weekend and watch Corabelle and me compete?" she asked.

"I'd love to," I whispered back.

## Chapter Eleven

## SHOW DAY

I was usually stressed* on a show day, but today, I wasn't. I couldn't believe it. It was always nice to have family supporting me, but it was so much fun to have a friend along with me, too, especially when that friend was Tamera.

Tamera helped us load Corabelle into the horse trailer and then she rode along in the truck with us all. We turned around a few times to check on Corabelle by looking through the truck's back window.

I was already wearing my dressage outfit when we got to the show. I started to feel a bit nervous, so I focused on getting Corabelle ready. I had braided her mane back at the stable, but now I groomed her and then put on her tack.

Mom and Lucy went to sign in Corabelle,

and they brought back our competitor numbers.

Tamera was great. She just stayed in the background and watched everything going on around her, and every once in a while gave me a thumbs-up.

And then it was time. I heard my event announced. Mom, Dad, Lucy, and Tamera all wished me a good ride and then Corabelle and I headed over to the ring.

When our number was called, I gave my wonderful horse a pat on the neck. "Let's do it!" I whispered to her.

We entered the ring and halted in the correct spot. I bowed to the judges.

Then Corabelle and I swung into our dressage routine. We had practiced it so many times that it just seemed to flow.

*Walk to here, turn here, now trot…*

Corabelle was such a pro. All the help Tamera gave us was paying off. I knew just what to concentrate on. I could forget that we were competing and just focus on helping Corabelle so

we both could do our best.

We halted in the exact correct place, and I bowed to the judges. Our ride was over.

I dismounted and gave Corabelle a kiss on the nose.

Slowly I came back to reality. When I looked over toward Mom, Dad, Lucy, and Tamera, I also saw Tamera's mother and father and Hugh. Wow! I couldn't believe it! They waved to me and I waved back.

The main judge stood up to the microphone and began reading out the results. First place went to a girl named Paula Sue and her horse, Paris. Then…

"Second place, Corabelle and her rider, Rashida!"

*That's us*—Corabelle and me! We placed second!

I gave Corabelle another quick kiss on her nose, and then I led her into the ring to receive our ribbon.

Afterward, my family *and* Tamera's family

hurried over to congratulate us. It was a wonderful feeling.

Tamera gave me a hug. "You and Corabelle looked amazing!" she said. "You're such a great team!"

"We couldn't have done it without you," I told my friend, hugging her back.

Then we turned our attention to the real star of the show—Corabelle! We patted her neck and showered her with praise. "I'm so proud of our ride and all we accomplished together this summer," I told her.

Corabelle's response? She twitched her ears and snuffled me with her velvety nose, like she didn't know what the big deal was!

# Chapter Twelve

## BEST FRIENDS

It was a few days after the show. Summer riding camps were over, and school would begin again tomorrow.

"Can you believe how fast the summer has gone, Rashida?" I asked her.

It was late afternoon, and Rashida and I were ending the day with a visit up to the top of Maple Hill, which was now *our* special hill. And this time we'd brought along a special guest, Corabelle!

Rashida's horse grazed while Rashida and I sat on the swing and talked.

"It seems like just the other day that my family and I were trailering Corabelle across the country," said Rashida. "Now we've moved into a new home, signed up for school, and settled in.

I've competed in a show, and I've even made

a new friend!"

She glanced at me.

"I'm really happy we became friends," she went on. "For a while there, I didn't think you wanted to be my friend. You seemed so different from me."

"Yeah, I thought the same," I said. "We're different in quite a few ways. What's great is that we figured out how to be friends anyway. Guess there are lots of different ways to become friends."

Rashida paused. I could tell she was choosing just what to say.

Then she pushed back on the swing, and as we flew up toward the sky together, she shouted out, "Not just friends. *Best* friends!"

# Glossary

*Many words have more than one meaning. Here are the definitions of words marked with this symbol ** *(an asterisk) as they are used in this story.*

**arena:** *an enclosed area for riding*

**assertive:** *confident and clear about what you mean*

**barrel racing:** *a sport in which a rider weaves his or her horse around a series of barrels*

**bay:** *reddish-brown color*

**benefit of the doubt:** *to decide to believe someone, even if you aren't sure he or she is being truthful*

**board:** *pay to keep a horse in a stable which provides space, care, and feeding for the horse*

**boutique:** *a small shop that sells fashionable clothes, shoes, or jewelry*

**canter:** *movement of a horse at a pace that is faster than a trot*

**cognitive:** *connected with thinking or intellectual activity*

**competition:** *a contest or challenge*

**confiding:** *telling something to someone that you don't want anyone else to know*

**contractor:** *a person who is hired for construction of a building*

**demonstration:** *showing how to do something*

**diagonals:** *straight lines set at angles*

**dismount:** *to get down (from a horse)*

**emotional:** *having to do with emotions and feelings*

**flash memory card:** *a tiny device that can be used with a digital camera or smartphone to store photos or videos*

**graze:** *feed on grass*

**groomed:** *brushed, cleaned, and washed*

**halter:** *a harness put on a horse's head so it can be led or tied up*

**halting:** *coming to a stop*

**intense:** *having strong feelings and focus*

**internship:** *a short-term position, paid or unpaid, at a business or shop to get experience doing a particular job*

**lay of the land:** *an expression that means to get an idea of where things are in a particular area*

**let down [one's] guard:** *not be defensive; be relaxed and trusting*

**lunge line:** *a long leather strap used to exercise a horse*

**mount up:** *get on a horse*

**mucking out:** *cleaning out dirty bedding or hay from a stall or stable*

**oversee:** *watch over a job to make sure it is being done properly*

**personality:** *the type of person someone is; how you think, behave, or feel that makes you different from other people*

**physical:** *to do with the body*

**posture:** *the position of a person's body*

**precise:** *exact*

**promotion:** *a better job*

**prompted:** *helped someone remember what they were going to say*

**reins:** *straps held in a rider's hand to help control and direct a horse*

**saddle:** *a leather seat that is strapped onto a horse's back for riding*

**shorthanded:** *not having enough people or "hands" available*

**sidewalkers:** *people who walk beside horses, usually to help the rider*

87

**signaling:** *giving a direction*

**snuffled:** *breathed in quickly several times while nudging with the nose*

**special needs:** *difficulties people have that require them to need additional assistance or services*

**stressed:** *very worried*

**tacked up:** *fitted a horse with riding gear*

**therapeutic riding:** *riding on horses to benefit in many ways, such as improving coordination, muscle tone, or confidence, or to relax*

**tongue-tied:** *unable to speak because of shyness*

**trail rides:** *outdoor rides on horseback, along a path*

**travel bandages:** *cotton wraps placed on horses' legs to protect them when they travel in trailers*

**trotting (trot):** *movement of a horse at a pace faster than walking*

**unhitched:** *disconnected*

**weaving:** *moving in a winding or zigzag course to avoid obstacles*

# Write a Horse Story!

At Round-the-Ring Stables, Rashida is usually busy riding, grooming, or feeding her horse, Corabelle. But when she has some time to relax, she chooses to read. She always has a book with her, either a book about dressage, or a story about a horse or a dog.

With your friends, write a new story for Rashida to enjoy. It's really easy to get going. You mainly need a good imagination!

### Supplies You May Need:
Pen or pencil and notepaper
### OR:
Voice recorder

## List of first lines (you can change the names, if you want!):

1. Lorna had been looking forward to this day as long as she could remember. "Today, I get to ride for the first time ever!" she whispered happily to herself.
2. "I'm so sorry," Richard said to his mare. He stroked her soft neck and looked into her beautiful brown eyes. "I never thought this would happen."
3. "Come on! Come on!" cried Mehta, watching her sister riding her amazing horse, Skyjet. "Just one more jump! You can do it!"
4. The little foal lay on the floor of the stall. Slowly, slowly, he began to try to get up. His long, thin legs wobbled.
5. The judges were waiting. The crowd was quiet. Peter took a deep breath. "OK, Zero," he said to his dressage horse. "It's our turn!"

## Here's what to do:

1. Gather your group of friends and sit in a circle.
2. One friend will begin the horse story. He or she can choose one of the first lines provided here or come up with an original line or two, and say it aloud.
3. The next player in the circle continues the story, adding another line or two.
4. Continue around the circle as many times as you wish until the story is done!
5. Have one player be the "recorder" and write down the story as it is told aloud. Or have each player speak their lines into a voice recorder!

# The Power of a Girl

For every *Our Generation*® product you buy, a portion of sales goes to WE Charity's Power of a Girl Initiative to help provide girls in developing countries an education—the most powerful tool in the world for escaping poverty.

Did you know that out of the millions of children who aren't in school, 70% of them are girls? In developing communities around the world, many girls can't go to school. Usually it's because there's no school available or because their responsibilities to family (farming, earning an income, walking hours each day for water) prevent it.

WE Charity has had incredible success in its first 20 years. Together, we've built more than 1,000 school rooms, empowering more than 200,000 children with an education. As WE Charity continues to deepen its programming, it's focusing on creating sustainable communities through its holistic development model built on the five Pillars of Impact: Education, Water, Health, Food and Opportunity.

The most incredible part about this model is that roughly a quarter of WE Charity's funding comes from kids just like you, who have lemonade stands, bake sales, penny drives, walkathons and more.

Just by buying an *Our Generation* product you have helped change the world, and you are powerful (beyond belief!) to help even more.

### If you want to find out more, visit:
### www.ogdolls.com/we-charity

 *Together we change the world.*

WE Charity provided the factual information pertaining to their organization. WE Charity is a 501c3 organization.

this is **our** story

We are an extraordinary generation of girls.
And have we got a story to tell.

*Our Generation®* is unlike any that has come before.
We're helping our families learn to recycle, holding
bake sales to support charities, and holding penny
drives to build homes for orphaned children in Haiti.
We're helping our little sisters learn to read and even
making sure the new kid at school has a place to sit
in the cafeteria.

All that and we still find time to play hopscotch and
hockey. To climb trees, do cartwheels all the way
down the block and laugh with our friends until milk
comes out of our noses. You know, to be kids.

Will we have a big impact on the world? We already
have. What's ahead for us? What's ahead for the
world? We have no idea. We're too busy grabbing
and holding on to the joy that is today.

Yep. This is our time. This is our story.

**www.ogdolls.com**

# this is my favorite horse story:

_____

_____

_____

_____

_____

_____

_____

_____

_____

_____

# this is **my** favorite horse story:

_____

_____

_____

_____

_____

_____

_____

_____

_____

_____

_____

_____

_____

_____

_____

_____

_____

## About the Author

*Susan Hughes is an award-winning writer of more than 30 children's books, including picture books, chapter books, young adult novels, nonfiction books for all ages, and even a graphic nonfiction book. Susan is also a freelance editor who works with educational publishers to develop student books and teacher materials for a variety of grade levels. In addition, she helps coach and guide other writers in revising and polishing their own manuscripts.*

## About the Illustrator

*Passionate about drawing from an early age, Géraldine Charette decided to pursue her studies in computer multimedia in order to further develop her style and technique. Her favorite themes to explore in her illustrations are fashion and urban life. In her free time, Géraldine loves to paint and travel. She is passionate about horses and loves spending time at the stable. It's where she feels most at peace and gives her time to think and fuel her creativity.*

*A Summer of Riding became the book that you are holding in your hands with the assistance of the talented people at Maison Battat Inc., including Joe Battat, Dany Battat, Sandy Jacinto, Loredana Ramacieri, Véronique Chartrand, Véronique Casavant, Ananda Guarany, Laurie Gaudreau-Levesque, Jenny Gambino, Natalie Cohen, Arlee Stewart, Karen Erlichman, Zeynep Yasar, and Pamela Shrimpton.*